Love Yourself

Finding Your Self-Worth

Flairs and Glairs
Publication House

"Love Yourself- Finding your Self-Worth"

ISBN No: " 978-93-90799-57-2"
1st Edition
Language – English and Hindi

Flairs and Glairs
Publication House
Regd. Under MSME Act.

Disclaimer

This is a work of fiction and solely represent the thoughts of the corresponding authors of the articles. Our editors have tried their best to edit the content of all the authors and check the plagiarism.
All the write-ups in this book are unique and are only published in this book.
In case any plagiarism or error is found, only the author is responsible alone, and not the publisher or the Compilers.

Cover Designing and Book Formatting
Shubham Shah and Ishani Agarwal

Acknowledgement

I would like to express my special thanks of gratitude to all my co-authors and team members who helped me to publish this Anthology. Without your Hardwork, Love and Support, it would not be possible to publish the book.

We are thankful Flairs and Glairs Publication, without whom, this projectwould never have been possible. Moreover a special thanks to our beloved parents, relatives and friends for their continuous support and encouragement towards us in completing this book.

Once again Thanks to all my Co-authors for being a part of this Anthology and also for believing and helping me to publish this Anthology.

Co Author

Shubham Shah (Founder Flairs and Glairs)
Ishani Agarwal (Co-Founder Flairs and Glairs)

1. Aman Sharma (Compiler)
2. Shalini Soumya
3. Shree Ram Pandey
4. Ratnesh Paras Singh
5. Shivani Singh
6. Priya Kumari
7. Bhavana Manani
8. Akash Prajapati
9. Alka Devi
10. Sammy Kumari
11. Nikita GajRaj
12. Mohanapriya
13. Pragya Verma
14. SP Smruti Ranjan Pati
15. Jatin Gaur
16. Dharmesh Sinha
17. Sahina Ghugha
18. Drishti Bai
19. Sharvari Sangam Patil
20. Arya Ojha
21. Adrija Paul
22. Podder Alaktaka
23. Tuhina Sharma
24. Sakshi Jain. (1)
25. Harshita Verma
26. Sakshi Jain. (2)
27. Shazia Jabeen
28. Amritanshu Shreshth

29. Arju Mali
30. Debesh Prusty
31. Keerthana Suriya
32. Priya Das
33. Mausam Agrawal
34. Priyanka Batra
35. Adarsh Mishra
36. Jayashree Sahoo
37. Hemant Suman
38. Ankita Bhatia
39. Christy Gnana Deepa. J
40. Priyanka Varma
41. Mihika Mishra
42. Krishna Motwani
43. Hema Kirthiga J
44. Kalamkaar
45. Ankita Sahoo
46. Ishrat Jahan Noormohammed Khan
47. Hansika SR
48. Padma Srivastava
49. Devyani Neral
50. Vidisha Agarwal
51. Prakriti Shreshtha

Shubham Shah

(Founder- Flairs and Glairs)

Shubham Shah, an entrepreneur at "Flairs & Glairs" a brand with dynamics in events organizing and cultural educational pan INDIA, is a 26yrs old guy who recently has entered the digital platform of imprinting emotions. He has initiated with his own open mic platform to help budding poets and aspiring writers under his brand named as "Teekhe Zasbaaat"

He is a commerce graduate from the Bhagalpur City of Bihar.
He states Writing has impersonated him since childhood and he has now been writing for over a decade!
Cooking, on the other hand, is his passion! He also mentions, trying out new things just tickles him!
When asked sir, Why SPICY EMOTIONS?
He smiled and added, “agar jasbaat teekhe na ho toh wo jasbaat kahan” Spices are all that blends! So do his words!
As a chef, he presents to you his dish! Hot and freshly served! Taste it! Feel it! Enjoy it! You can also find his writing in the Book “Teekhe Zasbaaat” and 50+ Co-authored anthologies. With his passion to explore opportunities across Platforms, he is working with keen devotion and We wish him all the very best for his future ventures.
He is Featured in the **International Magazine De-Mode** for his upcoming solo novel.
He is **Approved by Ne8x for its Lit Fest,** and is a **Golden Star Awards 2020 Winner.**
He is an **India Book of Records Holder** for his Anthology **Satrang,** and has the **Grandmaster** title by **Asia Book of Records**, for the same.
He has also been featured in **Prabhat Khabar**, **Dainik Jagran** and other renowned Newspaper for his achievements.
He has also been awarded with **India Star Republic Award 2021.**
He has been a proud co-author to
India Book of Records (Title- Black)
World Book of Records (Title -15 Wonders of Poetries)
India Book of Records (Title - Aaina)
Vajra World Records Holder (Title - Gustakhi Maaf Hai)
High Range of Records Holder (Title - Gustakhi Maaf Hai)

Share your reviews on his

INSTAGRAM

@spicy_emotions
@shubham4shah

Or via email on

shubham2shah@gmail.com

To stay tuned to his work and opportunities follow his business Handles

INSTAGRAM FACEBOOK YOUTUBE

@flairsandglairs
@teekhezasbaaat

WEBSITE:

https://flairsandglairs.in/
https://flairsandglairs.com/

Ishani Agarwal

(Co-Founder- Flairs and Glairs)

Ishani Agarwal hails from the City of Joy, Kolkata.
She is the co-founder of her Community "Teekhe Zasbaaat" and Flairs and Glairs Publication.
Been a Compiler for 45+ Anthologies, she is in the process for more. Co-authored in 150+ Anthologies. She is a India Book of Records Holder, a Vajra World Records Holder, a High Range of Records Holder and a Bravo Record holder.

Approved by Ne8x for its Lit Fest 2020, and Literary Icon 2020. Also a Golden Star Awards Winner 2020.
She has also been awarded with India Star Republic Award 2021.
She has been featured by the National Magazine "Taree Zameen Par" with the title 'unstoppable'.
Also featured in the International Magazine DeMode for her upcoming solo novel, she is proud to write on social issues, and is happy with the love she is receiving.
Connect with her on Instagram: @Ishani_agarwal_quotes / @compilations_so_far

COMPILER
Aman Sharma

Aman Sharma is currently pursuing his Bachelor's in Maths Honours but he is most interested in expressing his thoughts through his writings. Having a very intellectual mind which has a deep desire to explore the truth and causes of life and it's dilemma. He has already compiled 2 books- “Wo MAA hi to hai” and “Dad: Father, friend and hero” and again he is also a co-author in about 15 anthologies.

YourQuote:
http://www.yourquote.in/aman_gaurav
IG: @aman_shaan

Love Yourself

If you genuinely care about someone, you won't let them ruin themselves.
It's as simple as that.
Don't use your 'supportive friend' excuse to justify your ignorance.
If someone in your life is living a self-destructive lifestyle, don't encourage them.
Don't stand on the sidelines and watch.
Do something.
Tell them they're worth more than that.
That they're bigger than what they're facing.
Tell them there are better ways to heal.
Better ways to grow.
Tell them they can be friends with better people.
Tell them there's no escape from reality but it only gets better if you face it.
Tell them they're killing themselves slowly by intaking drugs.
Tell them you love them and don't want them to get hurt.
Tell them that you care.

Tell them "LOVE YOURSELF".

Let's fight it all.

Come
With all your wounds
And every lie you lied to
All of your worries at night
With every mouth you punch
And with all the blood you tasted
And with every enemy you made
With all of your family burial
For every dirty act you did
With every drink, burn your belly
And every morning I woke up alone
With no goal,
Come with your losses
Your regret
And your sins
And your memories
And your secrets
Come on,
Let's fight it all.

Shalini Soumya

शालिनी सौम्या अपने नाम के भांति सुंदर, शालिन और व्यवहार कुशल व्यक्तित्व है| कहने को तो अभी ये ग्यारहवीं की ही छात्रा है पर इनके हुनर आसमान सा ऊँचा है| एक बेहद हसमुख और मनमौजी लडक़ी! जिसकी मुस्कुराहट कामयाबी को छूने को बेताब है और बस वो उस मुस्कान से अपने माँ का नाम अपने से ऊँचा देखना चाहती है| माँ के प्रति लगाव उनका आशीर्वाद और शालिनी की लगन इन्हें जरूर एक दिन ऊंचा मकाम देगी|

Hey, inner me.

Perhaps life tires you many times; maybe we will stumble and may not give you what you love. Maybe you will be forced to do what you can't bear. Maybe you feel that you have reached the end of the road and the doors have closed on your face and the ports have ended.

But you are strong, no one knows how long you are left alone facing your fears on your own and how many times you have overcome the long nights of insomnia of your age and health, and no one knows how much you tried and how much you fell and got up to not stop after all this way I know how much these attempts were taking from your energy I feel everything! I know that you are very, very strong because you have not yet fallen, the unknown faraway that I do not know, except for a few lines, I felt your courageous spirit through which you really thought about giving up? But you did not fall all this time Do not forget this, remember that you are the greatest God created on this earth and your heart is precious. Do not allow something to stop it. Remember to always remain beside the hope and in the path leading to your dream. Remember that there is a beautiful thing in every matter that you do not like and make sure that after all these troubles will come something you never expected it and you never dreamed of it! I promise everything will be fine, everything will be as you wanted one day, be sure to trust me, sure that everything will change, but do not receive your sadness and do not allow death to take part of your thinking because all this will end and pass and that sadness never lasts like your friends who did not last I hope that you allow life to return to your face and smile on it again, stop if you are tired but do not give up and do not stop doing something that you love. You have to fight a lot for yourself and for what you love, you will face a thousand obstacles that try to bring you down, hold on to hope and continue, and do not allow anything that makes you weak on the edge of your path. Smile, everything will end.

श्री राम पाण्डेय

श्री राम पाण्डेय एक विद्यार्थी होने के साथ एक सुलझे व्यक्ति भी है। जितनी ताकत इनके मुस्कान में है, उतनी ही इनके कलम से पिरोएं शब्दो में झलकता है। आप सोच रहे होंगे वो कैसे, तो यूँ समझ लीजिए की दोनों कातिलाना है। हँस के भी आप के दिल को घायल कर सकते और अपने शब्दों से भी।

Everyone is unique

How can you know the uniqueness of a person unless you love him/her???

On the surface he/she is just a number...
On the surface he/she is a student, a clerk, a station-master, a school teacher, a nurse, a doctor, an engineer, this or that.....

Now, if you are a doctor, you are replaceable; if you die, another doctor will take your place. The world will not miss you as a doctor; you will not be missed... But if we look into your deepest core as an individual, nobody can replace you... You are unique. You have never been before, you will never be again. Nobody has ever been like you and nobody will ever be like you; you are utterly unique...

This uniqueness is a gift of god, and this uniqueness can only be known in deep love because only in love you do relax, only in love you put your armour aside. Only in love you allow yourself to be indefensible. Only in love you trust that the other will not harm you, so you allow the other into the deepest and the most delicate part of your being...

Ratnesh Paras Singh

My name is Ratnesh Paras Singh. I was born on 1/11/1999 is in U.P. I am a positive person and I have written few lines on love. Hope you all will like it.

I am a Karate Coach and an International player by profession. I am thinking of doing something different and want to live a healthy and happy life with my entire family.

"TERE PYAAR ME DEEWANE HO GAYE HUM"

Jin Galiyon Se Aaj Tum Gujarte Ho Na,
Un Galiyon Me Hum Mohabaat Kiya Karte The.

Oye Meri Shehzaadi Tere Pyaar Ek Paigam Hi Bhej De Mujhe,
Letter Nahi To Ek Miss Call Hi Kar De Mujhe,
Hum To Puri Zindagi Loota Denge Tujh pe,
Miss Call Ke Sath Sath Ek SMS Hi Kar De Mujhe.

Maine Tumko Paaya Hain Is Duniya Ki Bheed Me,
Khuda Ne Tujhko Mujhe Diya Hain Rakhunga Tujhe Dil Me,
Tumne Kyun Nahi Abtak Izahaar Kiya Apne Pyaar Ka,
Tu Ek Baar Aitbaar Kar Main Saanson Ke Sahare Utar Jaunga Tere Dil Me.

Tere Mohabbat Ke Deewane Ho Gaye Hain Hum,
Tere Husna Ke Ghayal Aashiq Ho Gaye Hain Hum,
Mangta Hu Tujhe Main Mere Har Duaa Me Rab se,
Tere Saanson Ke Sahare Tere Rooh Me Utar Gaye Hain Hum.

Mere Pyaar Ka Izahaar Karne Do Zara,
Mujhe Apne Kareeb Aane Do Zara,
Karna Hain Mujhe Kuch Pyaar Bhari Baatein,
Tumhe Apne Dil Me Basane Do Zara.

Dil Ki Dhadkan Zubaa Se Baya Hone Lagi,
Meri Nazre Tumhari Nazron Se Ishaaron Me Kuch Kehne Lagi,
Hum To Aaye The Aapse Dil Ki Baatein Karne,

Aap To Apni Baaton Se Hi Hamara Dil Churane Lagi.

Teri Ek Muskaan Ke Deewane Hain Hum,
Tere Chahat Ke Parwaane Hain Hum,
Thodi Si Jagah Dede Mujhe Tere Dil Me,
Dekh Lenge Pura Sansaar Tujhe Duniya Mante Hain Hum...

Chhup Chhup Ke Ye Dil Tujhe Dekha Karta Hain,
Pyaar Ka Izahaar Karne Se Ye Dil Darta Hain,
Kaash Tum Meri Dil Ki Baatein Samajh Sakti,
Ye Tumhaare Siva Kisi Aur Pe Nahi Marta Hain...

Shivani Singh

Name - Shivani Singh
Father's Name - Mr.Dhirendra Partap Singh
Mother's Name - Mrs.Kavita Singh

Dad: Father, Friend and Hero

बिना उसके ना एक पल भी गंवारा है
पिता ही साथी है, पिता ही सहारा है।

ये जो मुस्कान लिए बैठें हैं
पिताजी की ,
पहचान लिए बैठें हैं ।

कंधो पर झुलाया, प्यार से कंधो पर घुमाया।।
पापा की बदौलत ही मेरा जीवन खुबसूरत बन पाया।

"पिता"
एक स्तंभ हो आप,
एक विश्वास हो आप,
आपसे है अस्तित्व मेरा,
पिता ये नाम हो आप ।...

किसी ने पूछा: वो कौन सी जगह है जहाँ हर ग़लती,
हर जुर्म और हर गुनाह माफ़ हो जाता है ?
मैंने मुस्कुराते हुऐ कहा, मेरे पापा का दिल

ज़िन्दगी जीने का मज़ा तो आपसे मांगे हुए सिक्कों से था,,
"पापा"
हमारी कमाई से तो ज़रूरतें भी पूरी नहीं होती....

मेरे अजीज हो आप,
मेरे सबसे अच्छे दोस्त हो आप
हर इच्छा पूरी करने वाले,
खुदा से बढ़कर हो पापा आप

Priya Kumari

I am student cum rising poet from, Muzaffarpur, Bihar.
Want to be a romantic poet.
My passion is all about writing and my writing is all about love.

"Smelly Love"

You smell like toffee
which is my smile key.
You smell like wine,
for you,makes me pine
You smell like pickle.
makes my tongue fickle.

You smell like tea
creates scenario of sea.
You smell like food
makes me selfish and rude.
You smell like morning
makes me feel you are calling.

You smell like day
gives me hope of ray.
You smell like night
gives the paradise sight.
You smell like dream
gives me happiness.

Bhavana Manani

Bhavana Manani is a senior student at St. Daniel's Degree College, a college affiliated to Osmania University, Hyderabad, pursuing Bachelors of Commerce.

A commerce student by profession and a writer by passion. She believes in "either do something that is worth writing or write something that is worth reading."

"Writing is a FEELING only a few can feel!" is what she says. She has contributed to various anthologies as a co-author. Some of them are "Wo MAA hi to hai", "Dad - father, hero and friend." Her dedication is what sets her apart from anybody else.

For more of her writings, visit;

Your quote: https://www.yourquote.in/manani

UNDERSTANDING SELF

We do notice what other people are doing!!
Don't we??
Ever noticed YOURSELF, falling in love with self??
Is self-love being selfish??

Well!!
Here is what I feel...
Self-love is enjoying one's own company. It can be like enjoying your favourite music, giving yourself a treat at a restaurant and many more such things.
In fact, there's a saying,
If you have the power to go alone in a restaurant or cinema hall, then you can do everything in your life.

UNDERSTANDING SELF
Identifying one's own abilities, being proud of them and appreciating the one's own talents instead of making a comparison with others and feeling low.

So, what it conveys is:
If we learn to cherish our own beauty, own talent, our ability to do something &
Try to learn from our mistakes
Our past experiences and finds a way to overcome the flaws in self... then
One can actually fall in love with one's own soul
And when this begins,
We would realize that the world is a better place to live in.

Why Self-love?
Self-love is not only important but also necessary because you are the only one who will be with spending the most of

the time with yourself till the end. So, make yourself a better personality to be capable of falling in love with self.

Off course, in the beginning it would seem impossible, later you may feel though not impossible but yet difficult, and then slowly you will love enjoying your own company.
And once this start happening, one will never feel lonely though out the life journey.

After all being self-companion is definitely worthy.
And off course, Self-love is not being selfish.

Akash Prajapati

Akash Prajapati is from Patan, Gujarat. He’s studying in B.A. (English) and likes to write poetry.

तू एक उलझन है,
सुलझाऊ या समझू तुझे...
तू एक गीत है,
लिखूं या लबों पे गुनगुनाऊं तुझे...
तू मोहोंब्बत है,
इश्क़ करू या अपना लूं तुझे...
तू अहसास है,
छु लूं या गुज़र जाने दु तुझे...
तू मंजिल है,
छोड़ दू या पा लू तुझे...
तू राह है,
चल दु या मोड़ दु तुझे...
तू ख़्वाब है,
देखू या तोड़ दु तुझे...
तू जिंदगी है,
जी भरके जी लू या छोड़ दु तुझे...

Alka Devi

Name- Alka Devi
W/o- Upendra Kumar
Hosue wife
Passion- writing

जिदंगी में सच्चाई और इमानदारी के साथ, हमारा साथ देने वाली हमारी परछाईं ही होती है। जो उजाले में साथ हो ना हो अधेंरे में हमेशा साथ खड़ी होती है। थोड़ा सा प्यार पाने कि लालच में हम जितना लोगों के पीछे भागते है, अगर उसका कुछ हिस्सा खुद के पीछे लगाया होता तो आज न सिर्फ़ ,सबसे बेहतर होते बल्कि इसके अलावा कई आंखों कि उम्मीद बने होते।

Sammy Kumari

Name- Sammy Kumari (Araditharaj).
D/o- Devanand Kumar.
Study -Graduating 2nd year.
Passion – Writing.

इतनी छोटी सी उमर में, जिदंगी से मेंने बहुत बड़ी सिख ली है।
या यूं कहे कि लोगों ने इतना सताया है, कि इससे अब निकलने कि ही ठानी हैं।
सिख इतनी ही मिली है -कि जिदंगी में बड़ा बनो न बनो, भला जरुर बनो।
जब किसी कि उम्मीद बनो तो हमेशा अपनी यही कोशिश रखो कि उसकी उम्मीद न टूटे।
क्योंकि शायद आपको पता न हो,लेकिन सामने वाले ने आपसे खुद को जोड़ रखा हो।
और आपका एक उम्मीद तोड़ना उस इंसान को तोड़ जाए।

निकिता गजराज

निकिता गजराज
MA economics
हंसमुख स्वभाव की धनी, समाजसेवी व्यवहार
अपने विचारों को बिना हिचकिचाहट बिना डरे सबके सामने रखने वाली

दो शख्स हैं मुझमें जो अक्सर लड़ते रहते हैं
आमदा हैं एक नई बुलंदियां पाने को
तो दूसरा खुश हैं इतने में ही

एक को परवाह हैं हर छोटी से छोटी चीज की
एक बेपरवाह बढ़ता जाता हैं ऐसे ही

गलत भी गलत नहीं हैं एक की नजर में
तो दूसरा रहनुमा हैं एक छोटे से फूल का भी

एक को फिकर हैं जमाने की क्या कहेगा ये
तो दूसरा बेफिक्र हैं चाहे लाख बुरा कहे कोई

एक को फ्रक पड़ता हैं सबके दुख से
तो दूसरा खुद के दुख में भी मुस्कुरा लेता हैं

दो शख्स हैं मुझमें जो अक्सर झगड़ते रहते हैं

Mohanapriya.K

Co-author Mohanapriya.K is a good writer from Tamilnadu, India. She has completed her Bachelor's degree in engineering stream. She has been a writer for one year as her passion. She wants to be a best compiler and curator in future. Yet she sincerely hopes that this writing journey of her will bring her many successes. She also loves singing.

Self healing is more important

We cannot always predict what will happen in the end with what happens first. So do not make a decision on your own before embarking on a journey or mission or in the short period of time following it. For that, do not finish the process halfway.

Yes, a good start is a good end - they say. But everything that happens in this world depends on our hard work and effort. So the beginning can be anyway, but we hope its end will be a good one. Because that decision depends on the time too. Never be afraid of retribution, sarcasm etc. do not be afraid to stop your trips to victory.

Because you know they are not true. If so why should you fear for them or why should you regret thinking about it. Speakers are a thousand, why? Lakhs, even crores will speak reproach about you.

Don't forget to love the nature

All living beings in this world go in search of pleasures.
And no one seeks suffering automatically,
nor does he desire it.
Happiness is hidden in even the smallest things.
And we find happiness in even the smallest things.
What could be the reason!
Happiness - whether small or large is happiness itself.

Happiness is important but its quantity is not so important - it is true in itself.
The sun is so beautiful to look at sunset.
I just have to say that you have to give both eyes to see that scene.
What a beautiful evening to stand on the terrace and watch the sunset!
At that time the sky and the birds searching for her nest would be so beautiful to see.

What a beauty?
How much beauty? - That scene.
Wow!
What a wonderful sound!
Look that sound comes by this autumn.
Trees hum a wonderful song.

Pragya Verma

Pragya Verma hails from Prayagraj, Uttar Pradesh. She is a poetess and a writer. She has done 79+ anthologies, and two international anthologies and currently doing two world record anthologies as a co-author. She is also compiling two anthologies named, "SHADES OF NIGHT", "In a Relationship with Success". She has a great interest in making paintings and doing photography. She loves to gain spiritual knowledge and tries to find peace everywhere. You can follow her on Instagram: @wordsofpragya

Feel Free

You are a bird feel free and fly,
Don't forget your worth and no need to cry.
This world is a sky fly as higher as you can,
It's your life; live it up as it's your turn.

Love your body; obsess with your soul,
Do whatever is necessary to perform your role.
Don't trap yourself in any cage,
Write your life's book and put magic in every page.

This world is full of lies, hate and wile,
Don't let anyone take away your beautiful smile.
Keep your head high and face the reality,
Open your heart and start living freely.

I write the pain I hide

Trembling hands, head full of thoughts,
Assembling words and tied up their knots.
Knew nothing about how to write,
Playing with words still used them right.

First time of writing was full of delight,
Blown away my darkness and filled it with light.
I wrote whatever I wanted to,
Filled all the love and pain I got and knew.

Heavy head, sleepless nights,
Killed my soul not once but thrice.
I write how much darkness is inside,
Hoping someone could see the pain I hide.

This lost and fragile girl,
Wrote her thoughts which turned out like a pearl.

SP SMRUTI RANJAN PATI

Sp.SmrutiRanjan pati, a boy from a small town Jagatsinghpur with big dreams and believes in the power of pen!
'Believing yourself & your dreams can make you what you think' & he strongly believes in this pure imagination.
According to him, writing is a way to express the thoughts of love, science & experiences. He started writing from the time when he didn't know what he was writing, either it was correct or not!
It became a part and parcel of his fast racing life!

(1)

Shall I Compare!
Shall I Compare!
You with other boys
Nope, you are my soul
You are my life
You are my laughing face.
I know very well I can't be urs
But what can I do
Whenever I see your face
I forgot all my stress
Starting from the time
When you are unknown to me
Yes, we are still unknown because
I know you but you don't know me.
You are like my life's single page
That is not written with any phage
But am trying to write something on you
And my pen stops whenever I thought you.
Is it Love or something else?
I don't know
But I feel for you
Many times I tried to message
"Hey, how are you"
But I fear to send because my message will not be seen by you.
Hey,
This is the last message I want to say you
I LOVE YOU.

MY SOUL MY BEAUTY

Your Beauty Can't Be Compared Your Smile Can't Be Admired

You Are Like
"The Daffodils"
Dancing & Singing
With The Flow Of Wind

You Are Like William Shakespeare's Girlfriend Reveiled You Have A Such A Sweet Voice

That Feels Pleasure When It Strikes I Repeatedly Fall In Love

When I See Ur Eyes

Like Dna Replication It Replicates Without Ori Sites I Like Ur Cheeks When It Blushes With Pink

I Can't Say
I Can't Live Without You
Because
Life Without Soul Is Dead
And
The Soul Is You

Jatin Gaur

Hey, this is Jatin Gaur from Mathura (U.P). He has completed their graduation B.e.com (electronic commerce) at December 2020. Now he has started a brilliant journey of the writer's world. He likes to represent simple words, emotions, and feeling in a new way which people like most. He is only 19 years old, now writing is his passion and web developing is his career. He thinks if you want to live happy then follow your inner voice.

Love yourself

आप सभी को मेरा प्यार भरा नमस्कार, आज मै आप के सामने जीवन की एक ऐसी सच्चाई को रखने जा रहा हूं जिससे आप सभी वाकिफ हो कर भी अनजान हैं। आप सभी बड़ी शिद्दत से दूसरों को खुश रखने में निपुर्ण व्यस्त होंगे। परन्तु आप ने कभी अपने बारे में भी सोचा है कभी खुद खुश हो या नही। मै जानता हूँ आप सब का जवाब होगा हा बल्कि हम तो सब कुछ करते ही अपनी खुशी के लिए हैं। लेकिन अफसोश ऐसा हकीकत में कभी होता नही है। कभी-कभी हम अपना सब कुछ दाव पर लगा देते है हर हद पार कर देते है। तो इसमें हमारी खुशी कहा रही ? सोचियेगा जरूर!

सच्ची खुशी तो वो है जब दिल से आवाज निकले ये मेरे लिए था वाह मजा आ गया। लव प्यार मोहोबत एक दूसरे से करने में बहुत आसान होती है हम दूसरों के लिए इतने पागल हो जाते है कि कभी कभी अपनी जान तक कि परवा ना करते हुए कुछ भी करने को उतर आते है ।अरे मर तो सब के लिए सकते हो पर कभी खुद के लिए जी कर तो देखो यार खुद से मोहोबत ना हो जाये तो कहना।
"इस दुनिया मे आये हो प्यार करो एक बार नही बार बार करो किसी ओर से नही खुद से ही बेसुमार करो"
स्वार्थी होना कोई बुरी बात नही है और जब खुद के लिए स्वार्थी होने की बात आये तो बिल्कुल भी नही। क्योंकि यहा अगर खुद के लिए कुछ पाना है तो खुद को ही लड़ना होगा लड़ने का नाम सुनते ही अब हिंसावादी मत बन जाना।
चलिए आज मै आप को अपनी दोस्त की एक छोटी सी कहानी बताता हूं आशा करता हु अच्छी लगे और ना लगे तो भी पड़ लेना यार दोस्त की बात है। वो दुसरो के लिए बहुत किया करती थी।
"हमेशा उसका दुसरो के लिए लड़ना, सुनना, सुनाना, बात बात पर दुसरो के लिए खड़े हो जाना, बिना किसी के बोले ही मदत के लिए तैयार हो जाना सब कुछ करती थी। पर अक्सर वो खुद ही बुरी बन जाती थी सब की नजरों के सामने, रात होते ही कोने में छुप जाती

थी रोने के बहाने, दुसरो को खुशिया बाँटने चली थी पागल पर खुद को हमेशा खुद से ही नाराज पाती थी।"

तो ये थी मेरी दोस्त की कहानी मेरी जुबानी इसलिए पहले खुद को खुश रखो किया पता तुम को खुश देख कर भी किसी को खुशी मिलती हो।

Dharmesh sinha

धर्मेश सिन्हा वर्तमान में बैंक ऑफ इंडिया में मुख्य कैशियर के पद पर कार्यरत हैं। लेकिन वह अपने लेखन के माध्यम से अपने विचारों को व्यक्त करने में सबसे अधिक रुचि रखते हैं। एक बौद्धिक दिमाग होना, जिसमे जीवन की दुविधा और सच्चाई का पता लगाने की गहरी इच्छा होना, इनकी प्रमुख खासियत रही है। आजकल की दौड़ भाग वाली ज़िन्दगी में लोग जी तो रहें हैं मगर अपनों के साथ चाह कर भी नहीं जी सकते हैं। समाज के इन सब बातों को ही ये अपने कविता के माध्यम से उजागर करने की कोशिश करते है।

परिंदे पिंजरे के

ऐ परिंदे पिंजरे के
पर, तू मत फैला मत फैला।
क़तर दिए जाएंगे पंख तेरे
पर, तू मत फैला मत फैला ।।
किस सोच में तू खोया रहता है
तू तो लोगों का दिल बहलाता है
अपना दिल तू मत बहला मत बहला।।

ऐ परिंदे पिंजरे के
पर, तू मत फैला मत फैला।
बाहें फैला स्वागत करेगी मेरा एक दिन
उडुंगा खुले आसमान मैं एक दिन ।
बस ये सोच तू और मंद मंद मुस्का ।।

ऐ परिंदे पिंजरे के
पर, तू मत फैला मत फैला।
है अगर हिम्मत लड़ने की तुझमें ।
तो तोड़ पिंजरे जमाने से तू भिड़ जा
दूर कहीं गगन में फिर तू उड़ जा।।
लौट के फिर ना वापस आ
तू घर जा तू घर जा
ओ नांदा परिंदे अब
तू घर तू घर जा....

Sahina Ghugha

Sahina Ghugha is 20 year old B.Com student at Saurashtra University Rajkot. She is from Jamnagar city of Gujarat. She is state level winner in poetry competition 2017. She is Co-author of 10+ anthologies. She is an amazing writer and poet and she wants do something for society through her pen.
Insta ID: - Itz_Sahina_write

उसूल

मानते है कामयाबी उसी को मिलेगी,
जो रहेता महेनत में मशगूल है।
मगर घाव भी उसी के पैरो में दिखे,
जो चलने के लिए बनाता उसूल है।

तकलीफ कुछ ज्यादा ही देते है,
वो ज़ख्म जो मिलते बिना कसूर है।
आज वक्त भले तुम्हारा ही सही,
वक्त का बदल जाने का दस्तूर है।
यही सोच कर मुस्कुरा देते है हम,
की ये मुश्किल सारी फ़िज़ूल है।
सफर तो मुश्किल होगा ही ना,
वज़न बढ़ाने वाले साथ में उसूल है।

खुद के दामन को जो दाग से बचाते,
वहीं लोग लगाते औरो को धूल है।
उंगलियां दिखाते है दूसरों को,
खुद के गुनाह करता कौन कबूल है ?
कोई और करे तो अपराध लगे,
खुद करे तो हुई इनसे भूल है।
नए ज़माने के लोग है ये जनाब,
इनके कुछ ऐसे ही उसूल है।

Drishti Bai

A girl with many dreams
Ready for thrill anytime
Karma believer
Trying to influence other by being psychologist
Love to help others

A number of people will entry and will leave your life but you know what who stays? That's YOU in your life. We just try to change ourself because we want some special to stay but still they leave. After that, just filled with self doubt that we are not capable of anything but we forget it's not always you. Life will always test you by giving you conditions like just change yourself for the person and then blame yourself OR change yourself for your own sake.

An 18 year old girl named DIMPLE always being loved by everyone just because she always tries to keep everyone happy. She forgot who she was just she used to keep everyone happy. There was not a single person who loved her for who she is. All they care about was that she was there for them. She was not able to realise her mistake but god always send angel to angel.

One day on her way to home, she collides with a guy named ROHIT. His all books fell down and dimple started saying sorry. They both collected the books and rohit asked dimple for coffee. They went for coffee and became friends. After that, they started joining each other and became best friends. Rohit loved spending time with her, the way she was

When rohit started going with her friends, he realised that no one like her as person but he was not sure why they dont like her. Dimple's friend NIA met ROHIT and became good friends. Rohit asked Nia why they dont like Dimple and she told him how she changes according to people and rohit got manipulated.

After few days, Dimple decided to tell her feelings to Rohit that she loved him. When they met in a party, she came up with the news that Nia and Rohit are dating. After that also, dimple went to rohit to tell her feelings and rohit insult her by saying she is double faced person. She realised that all her friends are her enemy and there was not a single person who cared about her.

After that, she decided to be herself because in the end only you are there for yourself.

Sharvari Sangam Patil

She is trying to live her abnormal life normally. She is okay with not being perfect cause that's perfect to her. He believes everyone has a purpose of life. Some people spend their whole life for finding one.she is greatful to god that she found hers which is to write and help other to find their purpose.

I LOVE ME

I don't feel like putting makeup on my cheeks
Do what I want to do
Love every single part of my body,
Top to the bottom,
Pretending to be someone else
Is not cup of my tea,
But one thing is clear,
That I love me.

Is it a crime to love both genders at same time?
Am I committing any sort of crime?
I like everyone,
girls and boys too,
Sometimes I get confuse,
Should I use 'he' or 'she'
But one thing is clear,
That Iove me.

No matter where I go,
Everybody stares at me
Not into fancy clothes,
I am rocking baggy jeans,
I don't want to be someone.
That society wants me to be,
But one thing is clear,
That I love me.

One question roams in my mind
Whenever someone says 'hi'
Should i mention that I am 'bie'
I don't know
If world could see the way I see
I will love who I want to love

Cause this love is gender free,
I can not love boys only,
But one thing is definitely clear,
That I love me.

Arya Ojha

Arya Ojha is a poetess. She loves to write and recite poetry. Anchoring, Crafting are the other combination of her hobbies. She had participated in 15+ Anthologies as a Co-author and has compiled books named Elysian and Memoryland. Her Instagram handle is @writers_published where she has wonderful piece of write-ups. The Memory Land is her 2nd Anthology.

प्यार करना सीखो खुद से,
यार बनना सीखो खुद का,
मूल्यवान हो तुम भी इस जग में,
बातें याद रखो तुम भी।
महसूस करना सीखो खुद को,
कुछ अनजाने मत बनाना खुद से,
जानने की कोशिश करो खुद को,
व्यक्तित्व जानो खुद की तुम भी।
कमियों को गले लगाओ खुद की,
मजबूती से लड़ो उनसे,
अपनी ताकत को भी जानो तुम भी,
काम ना हो तुम किसी से।
अपने आप को खुद से परखो,
प्यार करना सीखो खुद से।

Adrija Paul

"Little hadn't she ever presumed that it'll be this important to her"

Adrija Paul is from West Bengal. She is a content writer on love, friendship and life genre since she was 13. She had been in the marketing team of Bestselling Author Arpit Vageria, she is also a published co-author with a publication house and she loves to pen her thoughts down rather than expressing her feelings to anyone - "introverted-extrovert"

She is basically a person who started writing about her teen unrequited love.

You can take a glimpse of her @__.adrija.___

प्यार तो बेशक था ।।

प्यार तो करते ही थे आपसे
आप शायद ही जुदा थे मगर दिल आप ही के पास ठहरा हुआ था।।
पता नही चला कब यह दिल संभालने लग गया अचानक से,
पता नही चला कब इबादत आपके लोए करने से आपसे करने लग गए।।
आजकल
पाया नही चला कब यह दिल संभालने लग गौए।
लकीरों में तब आपके इलावा कोई नही दिखता था पर आजकल तो लकीरें भी आपका नाम लेने से इनकार कर देते है।।
पता आज भी नही चला कब यह दिल संभालने लग गया था।
जहा दिल और दिमाग दोनो आपके नाम से वाकिफ़ थे
वही दिल, दिमाग, सरोर सारे आज आपके इन संयोग से इनकार करते है।।
पता नही चला कब यह दिल संभाल गया था ।।
पता नही
आपसे प्यार शिद्दत वाला था या ज़िद थी आपको हमारे पास रखने की मगर यह ज़रूर पता है कि चाहत बेइंतहां थी और शायद है।
मुत्तलिब था आपका प्यार, बेइंतहां शायद नही था जितना दूर यह दिल बोल रहा है और जितना यह दिमाग समझा रहा है आपको ऐसे बदलते मौसामो की तरह देखते हुए ।।

Podder Alaktaka

This is Alaktaka.
She is a student and a classical singer. She is from Northeastern part of India, Tripura Agartala and she is studying general medicine. She loves to write and read. She loves animals the most. She wishes to make her parents proud. She is a simple girl with vibrant dreams. Four years back, she started her journey of writing her thoughts into words. Still she is a learner who is trying to portray her emotions in words.
Insta handle: @evening_poetress_alaktaka

#YOU

I wish I could freeze this moment,
When I saw you for the first time.

My train was crossing over your city,
You booked taxi at the late hour of night
And
rushed to junction
to meet me.
The moment I met you,I felt such a spiritual connection between us.
Something so amazing and unique inside our soul,
that make me love you more.

When your cold hands touched my hand,
I felt a nostalgia flowing down my spine;
which created a sacred connection
without knowingly.

When I put my head in your chest
and
hugged You,
You closed your eyes shyly.
Then you caressed my hair on shoulder.

That moment I felt like my soul was always in search for you,
scorching like sunlight in darkness.
Like I always knew you.

Today when I'm recalling those memories,
a tear choked inside.
I wish I could freeze this moment right there,
but fortunately that moment gifted You to me
as my Soulmate,with endless happiness.
I wish I could freeze this moment in a
lifetime happy frame.

Tuhina Sharma

Tuhina sharma is from Jodhpur, Rajasthan. She is studying M.Sc. Zoology from J.N.V. University, Jodhpur. Co-author of two anthologies (Flames of life and Mithaas).
Instagram Handle: @diary_of_untold_feelings_

"खोल दे बाहें"

खोल दे बाहें ,
आज तु खुद को गले लगा ले,
खोल दे बाहें ,
आज खुद से तु प्यार जता ले,
खोल दे बाहें,
आज तु थोड़ा - सा मुस्कुरा ले ,
खोल दे बाहें ,
आज तु पंख फैला उड़ ले ,
खोल दे बाहें ,
आज तु थोड़ा खुद को जीना सीखा दे .

जिंदादिली

अनजान हूं मैं अपनी मंज़िल से,
बंजारों सा घूमू इन राहों पें,
ज़िद है मुझे कुछ करने की ,
सपनों के लिए मर मिट जाने की,
मंज़िल का मुझे पता नहीं,
मुश्किलों से में डरता नहीं,
अल्लाह की नज़र है मुझ पर हर घड़ी,
अब वहीं दिखायेगा मुझे मंजिल मेरी.

Sakshi Jain

Co-author Sakshi Jain is a good writer from Hathras
She has completed her diploma and currently pursuing B.tech
She has been writing poetry from 1 year as her passion.
She wants to be a self publishing author in future.
Follow her writings on instagram: @_shenu_writings_

Love yourself

काफी लम्बा सफर तय करके ही खुद को पाया है मैने
काफी झूठे रिश्तों का सच जानकर ही खुद को मजबूत बनाया है मैने
मैं जो कभी नही बनना चाहती थी लोगों ने मुझे वो बनाया है
किसी को खुश करने की जरुरत नही है अब मुझे
क्यूंकि अँधेरे में खुद को अकेला पाया है मैनें
वक़्त के साथ बदल जाना ही हक़ीक़त है
ये ही सच अपनाया है मैने
अपनो से ही सबसे ज्यादा दर्द पाया है मैने
और फिर उस वक़्त को भी तो भुलाया है मैने
सबको लेकर चलना तो मुमकिन नही है
इसलिये अब सबसे पीछा छुड़ाया है मैनें
पहले खुद को खोकर ही
आज खुद को पाया है मैनें
मेरे अन्दर की मिनी मी ने मुझे ये ही समझाया है
की तेरा तो कोई था ही नही
एक तूने ही तो बस तेरा साथ निभाया है
जिनको तूने अपना समझा था वो तो बस भरम का एक साया है

Harshita Verma

Co-author Harshita Verma is a good writer from Lucknow. She has completed her graduation in commerce stream. She has been writing poetry for 6 months as her passion. She wants to be a novelist in future.

LOVE YOURSELF

Before falling in love learn to love yourself
It will bring self confidence in your life
It will bring self respect for your identity
It will bring trust in yourself before anyone else.

Before taking decisions learn to love yourself
It will bring self sufficiency in your decisions
It will bring mindfulness in your life
It will bring courage in your heart.

Before pursuing the dreams learn to love yourself
It will bring hope to reach the goals
It will bring positivity in the path
It will bring encouragement at each step.

Always love yourself before anything else
Because you are the only one to help yourself before anyone else.

Sakshi Jain

She is Sakshi Jain from Roorkee, Uttarakhand. She was born on 8 July 2000.Her Instagram ID is @sakshijain_ writes.She is a patriotic girl .She is determined in her work. She works as a Co-author in 90+Anthologies.She is working as an Author in her Anthology"The Little Munchkin's" and “The Beautiful Tales of Love". She considers her family as her Strength.She wants to become a Writer in her upcoming future.

Dear Shizuka,

"Life is the Flower, for which Love is the Honey." Do you know this How much I love you? My baby girl. For you, I always get ready to fight with my friends Gian and Sumio. For you I can even die in Love.

I know you always take me as a Friend but for me you are my baby doll. I know I'm not like Degisuki. He is so intelligent and both of you have same intelligence and wishes.

I'm so stupid even I failed to solve simple mathematics questions. I promise u, I'll do lot of hardwork to improve myself.

I always promise you to keep you happy in every situation and I am always with you .You don't need to worry Shizu I'm yours only.

Please, be mine. I love you Shizu.

Shazia Jabeen

Name: Shazia Jabeen
Studying: high school
Institute: Sri Chaitanya Techno Curriculum

Be humble enough to realize you still have a lot to learn

Be ambitious enough to know you can be anything you want to be

Be easy enough on yourself to enjoy, to laugh, to have fun

Be mature enough to take responsibility for what you do

Be proud enough to take care of your body, your mind and your spirit

Be confident enough to see that who you are inside is more important than how you look outside!!

Be wise enough to choose your own friends carefully

Be absolutely sure that, wherever you go, whatever you do......!

"Just love yourself"

Love yourself first and everything else falls into line. You really have to love yourself to get anything done in this world." "The real difficulty is to overcome how you think about yourself." "You yourself, as much as anybody in the entire universe deserve your love and affection."

Be who you are and say what you feel, because those who mind don't matter, and those who matter doesn't mind." – ...
"About all you can do in life is being who you are...
"Always be a first rate version of yourself and not a second rate version of someone else." – ...
"If you cannot be a poet, be the poem." –

It does not matter how slowly you go, so long as you do not stop." "Try not to become a person of success, but rather try to become a person of value." "Just one small positive thought in the morning can change your whole day." "If I had eight hours to chop down a tree, I'd spend six hours sharpening my axe."

Amritanshu Shreshth

Master Amritanshu Shreshth is a student of Open Minds A Birla School Kankarbagh, Patna, Bihar std. 9 with an excellent academic performance and a distinguished skill in sports. With a magnificent start at the age of 12 he is an avid writer with a keen interest in life lessons and classical literature with some specific hobbies like playing guitar. He loves to express his feelings and life lessons with his write-ups. He had won many medal and certificates in Literature and Debates with his writing and speaking skills and had written many articles and science documentaries with his pen name Yuvraj.

UNSPOKEN WORDS

As truly said, "Words can either destroy or create a world". Words can either be the greatest strength or the weakness of a person just the difference being at the point interpretation and conceiving skills for different words and emotions attached with them. Words can be of many forms depending on the way we express or conceive them as they have different meanings keeping pace with the change in the expression. Words can either built a relation or break it, it can either give you success or failure and it can either make a world or destroy it just by its meaning and interpretations.

There are still many words and emotions which are not opened up to the world just because of the fear of the people's review, orthodox thinking's of the narrow minded people and many more irrelevant fear which needs to be ignored to be successful in this life combat. These unspoken words are either the one that need not spoken as they may hurt someone's feelings or needs to be spoken but the person is feared to do so thinking it be the unspoken words. These words are the most powerful words as they include the biggest truths and secrets of one's life. They may be either a boon or a curse for the world depending on the way of interpretation and needs to be opened up. If the emotions of a person is a tree then the unspoken words are its roots which are unseen but the most important and powerful part of the tree and one's life. Be the leaves of the tree and get the maximum sunshine and achieve success by flying colours and win the life combat.

They have become the windows that are never opened and have become no more than a wall that can't be opened. The unspoken words can be opened only if you are able to throw the pity fears about the world critics and prove that sometimes the unspoken words speak the loudest but to be clarified that these words can go unspoken yet your loved

ones can understand it. So, let these words be the roof not the wall and let them free, don't shy in any phase of life to express your words as they are the only path your emotions follow and give you a satisfied and loving life.

Arju Mali

She is a Student of Bachelor of Arts. She writes with lots of love, emotions and truthfulness. Her writings mostly Portray Courage and extend motivation.Her a Co- author of many Anthologies. Writing is her passion.
Instagram: @Arju mali25

खुद से मिल...

खुद में ही खुशी
खुद में ही दुःखी
खुद से ही परेशान
खुद ही से हैरान

होने वाली हर बात का
खुद ही जिम्मेदार तू
उन को सम्भाल कर
आगे चलने वाली तू

विश्वास भी तु, तू ही भरोसा
उम्मीद भी तू, तू ही आशा
सपनों, मंजिल, दुनिया
को पाने की आरज़ू भी तू

मेहनत कर आगे बढ
खुद को पहचान
यह संसार यह यश
तेरे नाम होगा

तू सब कुछ कर सकती हैं
अपने अंदर झाककर देख
तू पा सकती हैं सब
हिम्मत करके तो देख

खुदा भी देखना तेरे
साथ होगा
तू खुद से मिल

खुदा तेरे पास होगा....

"DON'T FORGOT TO SMILE"
"DON'T FORGET TO LOVE YOURSELF"

Debesh Prusty

This is like a dream for him but it is reality. This is the first time he stepped in to spotlight. It is never too easy to overcome the difficulties. He lays the foundation of his books from his college time. He loves to write all genres especially microtales. Too moddy, writing is his constant though

Loving yourself is the basis of life

Human's want is unlimited and hence they are running behind materialistic thing which never lasts longer. Nowadays everyone is busy impressing others and that's why they lost the primary goal of their own life which is to love them. There is a difference between happiness and what we describe as joy and happiness pleasure. On the other hand happiness is experienced in the mind and is therefore infinitely more powerful. Love fills a person with Nobel feeling, compassion, sympathy, sacrifice, understanding, welfare etc. The secret to happiness is to fall in love with you.

Don't lose hope if you lost anything. You can overcome the difficulties if you have faith on yourself. There are people undergo depression, failure and defeat, but there are some who determined to achieve success as they love themselves. Loving yourself can give you the moral support and confidence which noone can give it.

You are the one who has been through much still standing, love to the person who stand in your mirror. Atlast noone will be there for you, it is only you. Don't hate youself for being what you are not, love yourself what you are. You cannot make everyone happy, noone is perfect in this world so not you. Don't waste your time, energy, love on others because they are precious. Some peoole believe that loving yourself is just like selfish but truth is how can you love someone if you don't know to love yourself.

Create your best version and worth remembering.

Keerthana Suriya

Keerthana Suriya is a highly aspired, dynamic medical student, social-worker, a passionate writer and classical dancer who is engaging in self and social development, building relationships and exhibiting integrity. She is Co-Author of various other anthologies.

She is Founder of WACHC Foundation - Women and Children Health Care and also holding the position of Women's Health Empowerment Project Head in the trust Women's Renaissance Centre. She strongly believes that "When women and children rise, their communities and countries rise with them".

Follow her on Instagram - @keethusm

DON'T SEARCH FOR THE LIGHT

Wake up and first meet yourself
in the mirror daily.
Love the person reflected back to you
Tell something positive to yourself
Say to your inner self
"I believe in you,
You are smart,
You are beautiful,
I'll be your biggest cheerleader
Now and Forever
Let's stay strong warrior".

Don't search for the light
I repeat!
Don't search for the light
YOU ARE THE LIGHT

Breathe, be patient, and
trust the course of your life.
Be proud of everything
you have gone through,
and most importantly,
what you've become.
You have the power to turn
the miserable life meaningful
Be kind to yourself
Love and believe yourself
The rest will follow.

Priya Das

Priya Das hailing from steel city, Jamshedpur is a teenager with optimistic look to worldly life. She has co authored several anthologies and currently working on a novel. She is a great music lover and admires travel bloggers. You can contact her through Instagram - @inexorable_voice or email her at pdas72108@gmail.com

Dear self,

I know you are not doing so well mentally but you don't have to take any pressure. I am sorry for being harsh with you and highly appreciate your efforts. What you did today was commendable. It's never possible to change big things at a stretch, everything needs time. Taking baby steps towards it was never a mistake, it's all okay. It's okay to feel low sometimes; it's okay to be not okay. Life will frequently come to introduce you with new challenges, it will make you realise that half of them doesn't even care and half of them clap for you only after you reach the goal and at the end of the day you will be the only one to love your scars, your imperfection and if you are able to award yourself some kindness and love after all those shits thrown on you, fingers pointed on you, your character, your worth, your ability then you are a beautiful mature soul. Just be the way you are.

Yours
Inner soul.

Mausam Agrawal

She is 22 year old girl from Nepal and she loves writing poems, stories and shayaris.

Khudse Ishq

Khudse mohbbat karke jaana
Sukoon paya hai humne
Is ishq se sachi mohbbat kahan
Log hume khudgaraz kehte hai
Kehne do ishq karne wale aksar
Badnaam rahte hai...

Khudko banate hai
Khudke liye
Khudke liye khudko
Sajaya hai
Humne ishq ka dastur badal kar
Khudse ishq farmaya hai.

Priyanka Batra

Priyanka Batra
Introvertly extrovert
Loves reading
Always ready for adventure
Dream to explore every corner of the world

The word "selflove"looks like a show off word but we never realise how much important this word is in our life until such situations came when we have to upgrade ourself....
This story is about a girl named pearl she was a bit shy and takes alot time to get comfortable with new people...she got admission in new school,she thought she'll start a new beginning , new classmates , new friends but who knows that all her expectations will crashed down as soon as she started going to school... nobody talks to her , nobody likes her , her classmates starts bulleying her , she's all alone nobody was there for her and with all that she started hating herself with that much extent that she started to harm herself...she don't want to live anymore but she don't have courage to end her life also...
After 10th, she changed her school not just school but city also she wants to run far away from that school ,those people and maybe also from herself because now she's dangerous for herself , So she moved to a different city for her further studies...now she don't have excitement for new beginning but fear of past...there she met different kind of people and this time history doesn't repeat itself as this time she has lots of friends who appreciates her the way she is and then she realised that she did not changed herself but still people here like her just the way she is and then , she realised that people are different and their thinking too But above all the most important thing is to love yourself ..coz when people around you don't like you ..you need to love yourself the way you are..

Adarsh Mishra

I'm Adarsh Mishra.
Pen name:- Ansune lafz
I am a student of class 12th and also a good content writer (sayari, poetry, stories and many more according to your need)
Writing experience: - Fresher
"Likna hamara sok tha pta nii kb adat bn gai or dekha Jo apko to pta nii kb sayari ho gai"
IG: @adarsh_mishra_.official

Aaj kl ke es busy life me logo ko itti fhurst kha ki apne sath time bita ske thoda khud se pyaar jata ske Jbki ye sbse zyada important h, Eske alaba sbke liye samae h shibaye khud ke to kuch esi ke bare me likha h .

Dhyaan dijiyega!

"Aaj kuch Dil se likhna chahata hun
Khud se khud ke liye likhna chahata hun
Ab en kuch word's me es jindagi ko khul kr jina chahta hun",
"Khud se khud ko cha kr bs kathnai se ladne ki umang hogi
HAMARI JINDAGI BHI HAMARE TARIKE SE HOGI",

Ab suru baha se krte h. Jo ham sbko pyaara h " pr aaj kl ka bachpan to 3 saal me ktm ho jata h pr us samaye "APNE AAP SE PYAAR BHT JYADA H". Na piche aane or naa aage niklne ki hood hoti h ye bachpan hi to h jo ham sbko bht pyara h es samaye bs khud se pyaar or logo ke liye bhi bahi soch hoti h na kuch glt or na kuch sahi ki smjh hoti h bs "JINDAGI HAMRE TARIKE SE HOTI H" koi date to ek pl ruk jate h fhir dusre pl us msti ko fhir se dohrate h "YAADEIN BO BHI KAMAL SI HOTI H HAMRI JINDAGI HAMRE HISAB SE HOTI H".

Ab ham jb thode bde ho jate h es duniya ki aange niklne ki race me fash jate h kehne ko to ham me smjh aajati h pr sb kuch smjh kr bhi smjh nii pate h bs aakhe mund kr es andhere me kahi kho jate h ham to chalte rehte h pr kahi na kahi khud ko bhul jate h phir choti si chot lgte hi turnt muh ke bl gir jate h 2 pl khud se baat krne ki fhurst bhi nii hoti or fhir " YE JINDAGI HAMARE HISAB SE NII HOTI " khud ki kam logo ki zyada sunne lgte h logo se km apne aap se zyada drne lgte h self doubt ka kida kahi hamre mn me bs jata h kehne ko to sbke sath time bitate h pr khud ko bhul jate h or fhir kha apne sakar ho pate h jo tumne socha bo kha kr pate ho oro ki bt me aakr apne spno ko jala jate ho "JO SOCHA BO SB RAKH HO JATA H KYU KI TUMHE KAHA APNE SATH TIME BITANA H " social media pe sara bkt ese hi nikalna h "TUMHE KHA APNE SATH BKT

BITANA H" tumhe smjh ske tumhe esa person chahiye khud uljhe hue ho to ye soch kha se late ho
Dhire dhire ab ye smjh aane lgta h ki "KHUD KE LIYE KHUD SE ACCHA PERSON KAHI NII MILTA H " sara dispersion, low confidence, problems jhat se ud jati h jb "KHUD KI KAHANI KHUD KO SUNAI JATI H " hr glti tb smjh aajati h ab unhe bs fhirse nii dhohrana h "AB KHUD SE KHUDKO PYAAR KARANA H" hr bt ab phele khud ko batana h "KHUD SE.....

Jayashree Sahoo

Her writings started on yourquote, notojo and mirakee like writing platforms. You can search her on yourquote by name of Jaya Jayashree. Nowadays she is member of many writing communities and earned a alots of certificates through her writings.

She is Co.author of 160+ anthologies .Also she is Compiler of many anthologies in Hindi, English and Odia languages. Currently she is working as project head and board member of a reputed publication.

Insta id -@mixing_of_emotions
Email.id- jayashreesahoo665@gmail.com

Self love is wondering

If I love someone,
May be there chance of breakup,
May be there chance for hurting
May be the relation between us became fade,
May be there too much unknown question arise,
But If I love me or mine,
Without any expectation,
I get more satisfaction from me,
Noone there to hurt me,
Noone there to ignore me,
Only I search for self love,
Because If I love my self,
Sure the love became enduring,
Which is always wondering?
And I want it truly,
And in infinity...

Hemant Suman

Hemant kumar
Father's name - Late shree harishankar suman
Mother's name - Santosh suman
I am a student of B.A. 1st year.
Simple living high thinking
I love writing, reading and traveling and I always have a habit of writing only the truth.

खुद से प्यार करता हु मैं
जी हाँ पसन्द है मुझे खुद से प्यार करना
क्योंकि मेरी पसंद अच्छे अच्छो पसंद है
पर खुद से प्यार करना तब से छूट गया जब से वो जिंदगी में आई
वो मन मे ऐसी बसी की दूसरा कोई उनकी जगह ले भी नही सकता
पर जिनको में पसंद करता हु उन्हें शायद में ही पसंद नही
फिर भी पसंद है मुझे वो उनके परिवार से आज का ही नही मानो बहूत पुराना रिश्ता हो मेरा
उनकी हर अदा पर पता नही क्यो सिर्फ प्यार ही आता है
में चाह कर भी उनसे कभी नफरत नही कर पाया
हालांकि कोशिश बहुत की मैंने पर कभी कर नही पाया
उनकी तस्वीर दिल मे एक ऐसी अमिट स्याही से बनी है कि कभी मिट नही सकती चाहे वो मेरी जिंदगी में आये या न आये फिर भी ये दिल उनका ही दीवाना है उनकी एक तस्वीर ऐसी भाई इस दिल को की उसे शब्दो से तराशने का मन करता है
उनकी वो सादगी भारी फ़ोटो जब उन्होंने साड़ी पहनी
उस तस्वीर में वो इतनी अच्छी लग रही थी की उनकी में जितनी तारीफ कर उतनी कम है उनकी वो बालो की लटे जो चेहरे पर बार बार आ रही थी ओर उनका उन लटो का हटाना उसी पर उनके कान का झुमका का जिसकी एक अलग ही चमक थी उनके माथे पर लगी प्यारी सी काली बिंदिया ओर आंखों में लगा काजल ओर हाँ सच में उस दिन तो उन्हें काजल की जरूरत तो पूरी तरह से थी क्योंकि वो लग ही इतनी प्यारी रही थी इन सब के साथ उनकी सबसे अनमोल चीज जिसे देख कर हर कोई पागल हो जाये वो है उनकी प्यारी सी मुस्कान जिसे देख कर में अपना हर दर्द भूल जाता हूं मन तो कर रहा था कि उसी समय उन्हें कॉल करूं ओर सब बता दूँ जो मेरे दिल का हाल है
पर ये सोच कर पीछे हट जाता हूं की कहीं में उनके सपनो के आड़े ना आ जाउ हालांकि में तो ये चाहता हु की में उनके सपनों को पूरा करने में साथ दे सकू

शायद पता उन्हें भी मेरी फीलिंग्स के बारे में पर वो इन फीलिंग्स का हमेशा से गलत ही मतलब निकालती है फिर भी ये दिल उन्हें ही चाहता है ओर हमेशा चाहता रहेगा

I love u so much dear....

Ankita Bhatia

Ankita Bhatia a girl hailing from New Delhi persuing BSC second year and working as Immigration Consultant in real world and entrepreneur in virtual world.

Working to full fill her as well as others dreams by encouraging others and by providing them platform to showcase there talent.

Self Love

Thinking for others?
Take time for yourself
to think about your choices.

Thinking of how to let others grow?
Take time for yourself
To think what special you have and how to grow yourself in that field.

Stop thinking about others
Start giving time to yourself

Self love is the best to opt
Because no one knows you better then yourself

Christy Gnana Deepa. J

Christy Gnana Deepa, writer pursuing her Undergraduate in English literature in Madurai, Tamilnadu, India. She is a compiler of two anthologies, SECLUDED HEARTS and THE ARDENT HEARTS. Moreover, she is a co-author of more than 25 Anthologies. A writer by passion and a literarian by profession. You can follow her for more writeups in Instagram as ___budding___writer

SELF LOVE

Self love is the way of finding your pros and cons. It is the extreme state of analysing and interpreting your own self. Never hate yourself for any matter. You are the master of your own heart; you are the synonym and antonym of your own mind. You are the colour of your smile. You are the fruit of your success; you are the loser for your failure.

"Make the moment happy as happy you are!"

You are born to be happy, and share happiness with others. Love yourself, to make you happy always.

Priyanka Varma

She is Priyanka Varma studying Master's of Pharmacy from Visakhapatnam.

She wants to convey that - "Be proud of who you are, and not ashamed of how someone else sees you. Be yourself. You cannot truly love another until you know how to love yourself".

SELF LOVE

Self love is a revolution that every atom in your body is marching for.
Loving yourself is tough. Waking up every day with a proud sense of who you are can feel exhausting, or even impossible. But we all know, deep down, we can be the best versions of ourselves when we love ourselves fiercely and freely. Sometimes it takes mantras and prayers and sticky notes on the wall and chats in the mirror to make self-love stick.
You are not small.
You are not unworthy.
You are not insignificant.
The universe wove you from a constellation,
Just so atom, every fibre in you comes from
a different star.
Together, you are bound by stardust, altogether
Spectacularly created by the energy of the
Universe itself.
Accept yourself as a work in progress.
Continue to build yourself into the person you're dreaming to be;
The person you have all the potential to be.
Accept your flaws.
Accept your truths.
Accept your past.
And make light of them. no one can tear you down if you make peace with who you are and where you've been.
Stop being negative, focus on turning them into positives.
Focus on growing.

Mihika Mishra

My name is Mihika Mishra...
I am basically a student of 9 standard
Writing is my passion and that what brought me here........
I am not a professional writer but my writings are often heart touching.

Love_Yourself

I wasted alot of time in loving other, caring for them..... Alot of time actually......

Although I did so much for them
But in return I always got tears and heartbreaks.....
I heard people saying that love is the best feeling
But I never understood how????

May be cuz I loved wrong people
Because as per them showing love is equivalent to irritation........

One day I thought that if it is so difficult and expensive to get the love of others....
I decided to quit......

Now I started loving myself and now all those people who had once rejected me started talking to me...

That's the real power of Self Love.

Krishna Motwani

Krishna Motwani is a Student currently.
She use to pen down her feelings.
She is a moody girl.
She started writing in the month of June, 2020.
She writes in her free time.
She writes some motivational quotes or poetries too and practices artworks also.
She lives her life like a bird
As bird flies freely and enjoys life like that she also lives her life freely and enjoy fullest.
For motivating and inspiring poems and quotes, you can check her on instagram: @ unique__blog_

कदम कदम पर कठिनाइयाँ आएगी, जो तुम्हें मंजिल तक जाने के लिए रोकेगी।

तुम मुश्किलों का सामना करो,
किसी भी मोड़ पर मत डरो।

मंजिल तक का रास्ता है काटों से भरा,
पहुचोगे तब ही तो होगा तुम्हारा सपना पूरा।

हौसला है एक किनारा,
इसे कभी तोड़ना मत वरना रह जाएगा सपना अदूरा।

कितनी भी मुश्किलें आए, उनका सामना करना है,
अपनी ख्वाहिशों के लिए हमें लड़ना है।

हिम्मत हार जाओगे,
तो कैसे आगे बढ़ोगे!

भूल जाओ बीते हुए कल को,
नई उम्मीदों के साथ नई शुरुआत करनी है तुमको।

ये सब हमारी जिंदगी का हिस्सा है,
समझो जैसे चंद पलों का किस्सा है।

Hema Kirthiga J

She is Hema Kirthiga J, and her pen name is sparkle. She is professionally a psychologist and passionately a writer. She heals others but writing heals her. She is writer, reader, orator and a believer. She is from Chennai. She lives by the principal of inspire and be inspired. She writes her heart and soul and she deeply believes that the depth of her heart and the nib of her pen are soulfully connected. Writing is an art and she is a proud artist. She loves what she does and loves what she writes. You can reach her at

Instagram- @the_pen_queen

Email- inker.sparkle@gmail.com

Yourquote – JKM

I AM THE BEST!

I know I have flaws,
I know I have few bad characters,
I know I am not all good,
But then its okay,
I have to accept myself,
I have to love myself,
Only I can play my role in a best way,
Who else can?
Even if I don't love myself?
Who will?
If I don't live for my self?
Who else will?
I know I am not perfect,
But I don't have to be perfect,
My flaws will shine,
My heart will win,
I love myself,
That's what the first step i took,
For a better life,
For a better change.

Kalamkaar

This is Kalamkaar. He is from Uttrakhand bought up in Meerut (Up). His hobbies are reading and writing. His interest is in writing. He loves writing. He is part of 295+ Anthologies as Co-Author. He won 290+ Certificate in Writing, He Start writing 29 February 2020. He is part of 4 anthologies as Co Author going for record and He is omg record holder as Co -Author of Book Called Laposia. He is part of 6 international Anthologies as Co - Author. He is simple and people observer. His insta handle is kalamkaar51 and email is kalamkaar51@gmail.com. He believes in Karma.

खुद से प्यार करें

चाहें कोई भी तुमसे दूर जाये, उसकी ना परवाह करें!
दे खुदको प्राथमिकता पहले चिंता अपनी पहले स्वयं करें!
किसी के पीछे ना भागे ना उसको सीमा भूल जाने की छूट दे!
दे इज़्ज़त आपको और आपके फैसले का सम्मान करें!
मौसम की तरह ना बदले और ना आपके बूरे वक़्त में हाथ छोड़कर चला जाये!
रिश्तो में ना उलझे निकले वो हल जिससे जो उलझा हैं वो सुलजे!
मान आपका हर जगह हो आपकी बातो को भी माने लोग ऐसा आपका व्यक्तित्व हो!
दूसरे से पहले अपने बारे में सोचे, ख्यालात अपने दूसरों के प्रति अच्छे रखे!
जो ना दे महत्वता वहाँ ना रुके बेवजह किसी के आगे ना झुके!
अपनी भावनाओं को संभाल के रखे कोई ना उठाले फायदा इसका भी ख्याल रखे!
भावनाओं में ना बहे बाते सबके समक्ष खुलकर कहे!
बनाले अपने को इतना प्रभावशाली के आपके बिना कोई ना रहें!
बाते सारे आपसे हर कोई कहे, बिछड़ने अगर आपके हर किसी के अश्रु बंदीदो से बहे!
जो करना कद्र आपकी उससे कभी ना इज़हार करें!
कद्र करें अपनी अपने पर विशवास करें, और खुदसे प्यार करें!

Ankita Sahoo

Hii lovely people out there she is Ankita Sahoo. She is currently doing her graduation in political science. She is an introvert and a bookworm by nature. She is even a writer and is extremely passionate about penning her thoughts. Her goal is to serve her nation by being an IAS officer.

Focusing on one's own self is very important; in this world where people promise to their respective partners to love them unconditionally for their entire life, they tend to forget that self-love also can't be neglected. Self-love is the key to self-confident, which makes the foundation towards success. Keeping yourself at the first place is not about being selfish rather it's all about loving yourself. Most of the problems are solved, most of the question are answered effortlessly once you start believing in yourself and loving, caring for yourself. Self-love is not optional it's necessity.

Ms. Ishrat Jahan Noormohammed Khan

Ms Ishrat Jahan Khan is a passionate Teacher and a Writer she loves reading and writing. Loving and caring is her hobby. And keep learning and accept the positive suggestion is her quality.

She belongs to North India and stays at Ulhasnagar (Maharashtra).

Loves humanity always.

Love yourself

Life you get once
So don't be tense
Have always hope
And a wide scope

Your best friend is you
It's you who can help you
Self is a important
Self is a competent

Self is love
Self is like dove
Self is lifeline
Self is shine

Life is to enjoy
It's to reply
Make it happy palm
And be always calm

Hansika SR

Hansika SR is a Chartered Accountancy student, also pursuing BCom (Acc/Fin) and a Carnatic singer by profession and a passionate writer, poet, a rhetoric public speaker and an enthusiastic learner of Vedic scriptures. She has brought numerous laurels through her versatility and her linguistic skills, is now a part of more than 15 anthologies. She is a consistent blogger and quote writer on mirakee, yourquote and blogger.

Solitude

It's painful, yet another pavement.
It's soulful, yet yearns attachment.
It's cold, yet looks out for warmth.
It's bliss, yet gruelling.
It's that smile, yet has painful frowns.
It's filled with richness of peace, yet a war.
It's self infiniteness, yet lonelier.
It's limitless experience, yet bitter.
It's a miracle from within, yet mysterious.
It's soft and mellifluous, yet louder than a scream.
It's a fly all alone, yet stronger than in a crowd.
It's new and sole, yet another voice of the soul.
Listen your inner voice when lonesome,
Earn the thrust of your soul, so wholesome.
For, it's an unheard melancholy of soul's etude
With gratitude, cherish your solitude!

Padma Srivastava

Padma Srivastava, a student of Archaeology with it she is also a good writer and singer. She is very passionate about her future and works. She is heartily attached with Varanasi and started writing from the age of 13year. She has been co _author of several anthologies till now. Her first anthology got published in TITLI from flairs and glairs publication.

खुद से इश्क़ है हो रहा

कमियां महसूस होती नहीं अब किसी की
लगता है खुद से इश्क़ होने लगा है
बढ़ रहीं हूं हर एक सीढ़ियों पर आगे
शायद मुझे कोई खोने लगा है
सताती नहीं अब तो नींदें भी रातों को
कहीं मेरा ही ख़्याल मुझमें सोने लगा है
था जिन ग़मों से बड़ा प्यार मुझे
वो अन्दर ही अन्दर कहीं रोने लगा है
खुशियां लगी हैं कदम रखने दिलों में
शायद अब हर ग़म सर पर मुस्कान ढोने लगा है
हर ज़ख्म जो थे चोट पहुंचाते दिलों को
अनदेखा सा मुस्कुराहट उसे धोने लगा है
ख्वाबों की चादरें अब ओढ़ने की इच्छा ही नहीं
हर दिन बीतने लगे हैं एक ख्वाब जैसे
हर किस्से तो अब ऐसे लगते हैं
हो कोई खुली किताब जैसे
आंखों में हैं नींदों का पहरा छाया
सदियों से जगी हो रात जैसे
अब लगती नहीं ज़रुरत किसी की
मैं ही मौसम, मैं ही बरसात जैसे
हर पल अब खुश रहने लगी हूँ
हो हर पल कोई साथ जैसे
दुनिया चाहे अब कुछ भी करे
खुश हैं हम खुद में ही
चाहे भले दुनिया को रश्क़ हो जैसे
अब न पड़ता है फ़र्क किसी से
खुद से इश्क़ हो रहा हो जैसे।।

Devyani Neral

She is a co-author of 50 anthologies and a published poet 24 years of her age has given her innumerable thoughts to write. She is an engineer by profession and a writer by passion.Reading thrills her and feels her with joy and so does writing. She is currently writing her first book which will be of self - help genre. Motivational writings are her cup of tea. She strongly believes that we are here to write our own story and create our own path.

Lost but Found

I am lost in a crowd,
where no one recognises me.
Seems that sun will debare me from it's sunshine.

But why do you want to be found?
Why do you want someone else's recognition?
Why can't you find yourself within you?

It's upto you to grab that sunshine.
It's upto you to recognise yourself.
It's upto you to bloom in that crowd.
And finally it's upto you to shine in the sunshine.

Vidisha Agarwal

She is an amazing artist,creative writer,passionate dancer and a very good cook.

Love Yourself

Love Yourself;
Trust Yourself;
Believe in yourself;
Speak for Yourself;
Face Yourself;
Answer Yourself;
Be Yourself.
Trace the Map to your Soul
Check whether your Persona
Coincides with it…?
Peep inside your Magic Shop,
You'll get the Best of You
It's you, only you
Who can chase out
The Best of you.
Self realization,
And you'll Glow like a Dream,
A Brand New Day awaits you.
Love Yourself;
Trust Yourself;
Believe in Yourself;
Speak for Yourself;
Face Yourself;
Answer Yourself;
Be Yourself.
Oh my isn't it wonderful?
Feel this Euphoria,
When reality becomes Utopia.
The Shadow like you
Too has it's Inner Child
Huh, Singularity? So What?
Crush that Love Maze.
Stay Gold!
….cause
We have to be
Eternally Bulletproof.

Prakriti Shreshtha

Miss Prakriti Shreshtha is a student of St. Joseph's Convent High School, Bankipur Patna in Std.10 with exemplary academics. She is an avid reader and has keen interest in Greek classical literature. She started written poems, short stories at the age of 12 with the pen name Tidal Seashell. She loves to convey her emotions through poetry and quotes. She adores the Greek god Apollo who is the Olympian God of sun and light, music and poetry, prophecy and knowledge, order and beauty. As she cherishes all forms of art, some of her hobbies are sketching and singing.

She has won numerous prizes for her art works. Despite of all the struggles in life she hopes to pursue her dreams through her constant hard work.

BETRAYAL

Moon shone in the night sky,
When I heard a terrible lie.
"Tomorrow we'll have fun,
A little away from the shinning sun."

A minute before with my wings I flew ,
Now I'm gone without any clue.
Thirteen years was my days of rest,
I never knew what came next.

When my hopes were shattered down,
When I became mere a clown.
I was a happy hearted girl too young,
With my sweet voice day and night I sung.

Then I met someone strange,
Our friendship reached high range.
Once we went hand in hand,
To a beautiful distant land.

My eyes were filled with tears of joy,
My clutch tightened on my toy.
Sweet smell of Hyacinth filled the plane,
Shining like pearl were drops of rain,

I chocked back a sob,
Cause I knew I could open my heart's knob.
Just then something struck my head,
And I noticed bloodshed.

I noticed a grin to sly,
And I sensed the Terrible Lie.
My body became numb,

And I felt dumb.

The injury was intricate,
But betrayal was something my heart couldn’t take.
So I chose to end the pain,
And allowed my soul to drain.

Flairs and Glairs, a platform by a student for the students. We are esteemed youth struggling to carve out our path for our future and we follow a basic mindset Since everyone is not born with all-round skills. Joining hands with people who are born to execute it with perfection is the best way to evolve. Self-Evolution is the need of the hour but, evolving as a community is what we strive for. The initiative as kickstarted by, Founder- Mr. Shubham Shah with the motive to utilize the skillset and talent of writing has now a team of 10+ people who are actively participating into newer forms of learning and discovering talents among youngsters. We Provide platform and services like Publishing opportunities, Open mics, Workshops, Hands-on training. Operating with Brand Name of Flairs and Glairs (Publication House), we offer the chance of elevating a passionate writer to an esteemed author With Brand name Teekhe Zasbaaat. We bring to you an opportunity to get accustomed with the Public Speaking and Presenting of Thoughts along with regular challenges to brush up your inking spirit. The newest initiative to extend our services we introduced in a new writing Platform- The Glittering Fables and Ink Over Tears.

We Choose to Fly Like A Falcon than to be

a Leg Pulling Crab.

To Know More: Infoline – 7781900870
Mail Us At-
flairsandglairs@gmail.com / info@flairsandglairs.in
Or Visit is at
www.flairsandglairs.com / www.flairsandglairs.in
Social Handles- @flairsandglairs @teekhezasbaaat

www.ingramcontent.com/pod-product-compliance
Ingram Content Group UK Ltd.
Pitfield, Milton Keynes, MK11 3LW, UK
UKHW022005190726
13853UKWH00004B/1739

9 789390 799572